How to Help a Friend

For Dr. Kris Zegocki, Clinical Nurse Specialist Karen Bennett,
and all the amazing staff at Whipps Cross Hospital and
St. Bart's Hospital, London—thank you!
KN

For Farheen, Rachel, and Emilie. Thank you for the
countless years of love and support!
CA

Text copyright © 2021 by Karl Newson
Illustrations copyright © 2021 by Clara Anganuzzi

First US edition 2022
First published by Studio Press, an imprint of Bonnier Books UK, 2021

Library of Congress Catalog Card Number pending
ISBN 978-1-5362-2667-6

22 23 24 25 26 27 TLF 10 9 8 7 6 5 4 3 2 1

Printed in Dongguan, Guangdong, China

TEMPLAR BOOKS
an imprint of
Candlewick Press
99 Dover Street
Somerville, Massachusetts 02144

www.candlewick.com

How to Help a Friend

Karl Newson

illustrated by
Clara Anganuzzi

templar books
an imprint of Candlewick Press

Some friends need a great big hug

to feel that all is well.

Some prefer to be alone.

Some listen.

Others tell . . .

the most

adventurous stories

of the times

that came before!

Some friends may not want
to talk about it anymore.

Some friends need a little help before their **smiles** can form.

It could be in the rising sun.

It might **be** in a storm.

Some friends like
to read a book,

and some friends
like a bath.

Some just want to watch TV,

while others need to laugh.

Some friends

have a list of things

they'd like to try to do.

Some friends will be happiest
just to be with you—

sitting, doing nothing much,
and saying not a word.

Sometimes just a tiny smile
will let them know you've heard.

Some **friends** keep a diary.

Some **friends** write a letter.

Some will sing their favorite songs to help themselves feel better.

Some **friends** say a **flower** helps a heart that has an ache.

Some prefer some ice cream and a lot of chocolate cake!

Some **friends** don't want anything except to just feel sad.

Some **friends** want for **all** the things
they wish that they still had.

Some **friends** want to go back home.

Some may want to

SHOUT!

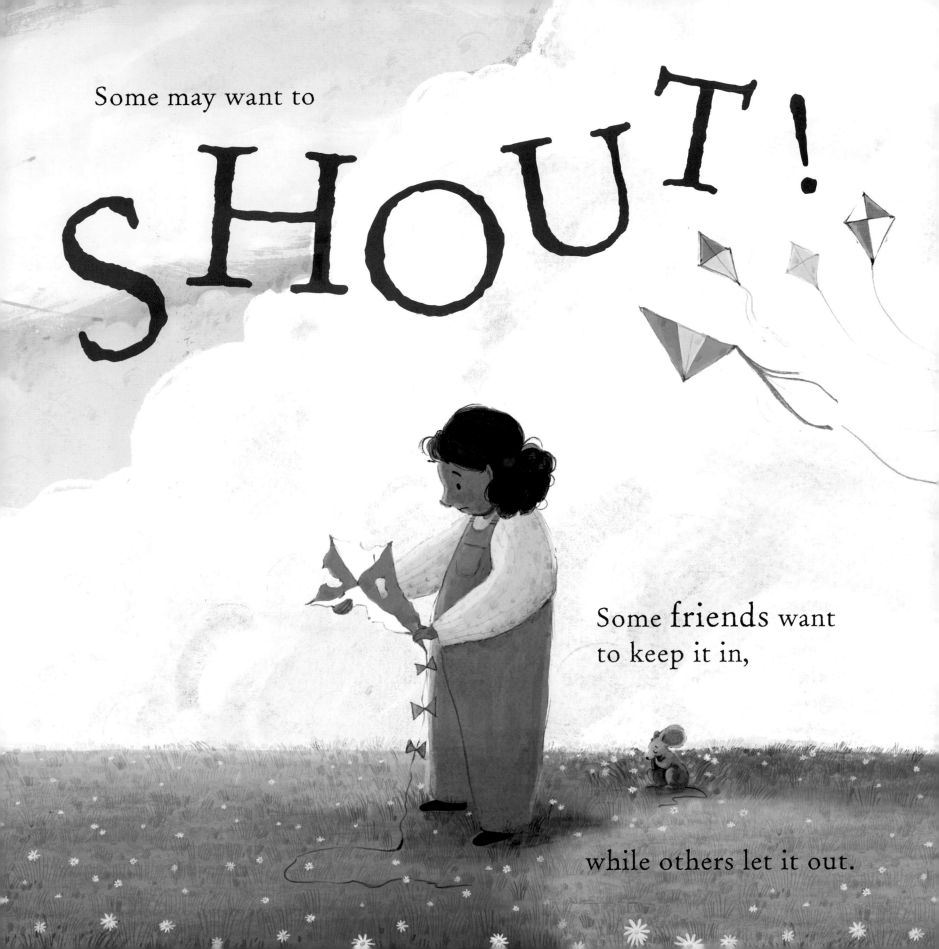

Some friends want
to keep it in,

while others let it out.

Some friends like to share their hearts
to show you that they care.

Some friends like to send a note
to let you know they're there.

Some friends will be with you,
whether they are near or far.

Some friends will be
there for you
no matter where
you are.

Some friends will grow old with you.

Some may come and go.

Some will teach you things about yourself you didn't know.

Some friends might need **comforting**
to help them to feel good.

Some
    might
        want to
            run it
                off

around the neighborhood.

Some friends want to fly away.

Some
friends
want
to hide.

Some friends might want someone else
but appreciate you tried.

And maybe, in a while,
they'll be **happy** you were there . . .

All of us are different.
Everybody.
Everywhere.

Some friends
need a lot of friends
to help them see
things through ...

You can be the greatest friend
just by being you.

This story was written in the middle of my cancer treatment. Although it was a difficult time in my life, I found myself filled with a feeling of constant love and support from all those around me, from my partner who was there with me every single day, to my doctors, nurses, and all the amazing staff who lifted me up and found time to get to know me and enjoy a laugh. My family filled me up with support and love, and my friends, both old and new, reached out and gifted me with daily messages of support and cookies and a whole herd of elephant illustrations that I will treasure for all my days.

This story is all those feelings, wrapped up together and sent with a great big hug.
It's my thank-you to my friends and family for helping me through. I'd also like to say a special thank-you to Clara Anganuzzi for bringing my words to life so wonderfully, and to the brilliant team who published me.

I hope the story helps anyone who needs it and reassures the reader
that just being yourself is as perfect as you can be.

Karl Newson